In a final effort to perk Oddly up, Darren takes him round to
see his friend Keith. Oddly catches sight of Keith's keyboard,
and a star is born. Oddly may not have been programmed
to play music, but he's certainly going to have a good try.

There are lots of laughs along the way as Oddly struggles
with his feelings, his music – and his rival, the fantastically
accomplished robot Perfectly. Will his emotion overcome
him, or can he pour it into that humming, buzzing, totally
amazing Melody of Oddly?

Jon Blake was brought up in Southampton and he has
worked as a community centre warden, a teacher and a
furniture salesman. Now, in addition to writing, he is a part-
time community worker and lives in Cardiff.

By the same author

ODDLY

Jon Blake

THE MELODY OF ODDLY

Illustrated by John Farman

PUFFIN BOOKS

PUFFIN BOOKS

Published by the Penguin Group
Penguin Books Ltd, 27 Wrights Lane, London W8 5TZ, England
Penguin Books USA Inc., 375 Hudson Street, New York, New York 10014, USA
Penguin Books Australia Ltd, Ringwood, Victoria, Australia
Penguin Books Canada Ltd, 10 Alcorn Avenue, Toronto, Ontario, Canada M4V 3B2
Penguin Books (NZ) Ltd, 182–190 Wairau Road, Auckland 10, New Zealand

Penguin Books Ltd, Registered Offices: Harmondsworth, Middlesex, England

First published 1992
1 3 5 7 9 10 8 6 4 2

Printed in England by Clays Ltd, St Ives plc

Chapter One

Months have passed since I visited Aunty
Beth and first met her robot butler, Oddly.
Mum and Dad had gone on holiday, so
Aunty Beth gave him to look after me. He
was great for cooking meals, cleaning and
switching the telly over. The problems
started when my friend Jackie programmed
Oddly with feelings. But after a few
adventures, we became good mates.

At first, Mum and Dad were quite
happy to have Oddly around. He helped
out with the housework, his manners
were perfect, and, best of all, he didn't
need feeding. The trouble was, he didn't
have a job. He was programmed to be a

butler, but he'd decided he didn't like being ordered around. That left him at a loose end. He began to spend more and more time in his airing cupboard. He started getting up at two, then four, then eight, then just in time to go to bed again. He forgot how to do the simplest things, and spent all his waking hours watching telly, because he wasn't too sure how to get out of the chair.

Mum and Dad got more and more impatient. They hadn't got jobs either, so the last thing they needed was Oddly dragging them down. One day, Dad got so fed up, he switched off the telly, just to see what Oddly would do. For a while, Oddly sat watching the blank screen. Then he moved his chair a few inches and began to watch Dad.

It was the last straw. When I got home from school, Mum had a serious word

with me. "Either you find Oddly
something to do," she said, "or
somewhere else to live."

"He can't help it," I protested. "His
batteries are running down."

It was only an excuse, but the moment
I said it, I wondered if it was true.

"Will you buy him some new ones?" I
asked creepily.

Mum scoffed and showed me the holes
in her slippers. I didn't bother arguing. I
hated being poor and not being able to

buy the stupidest little things. If I wanted batteries, I'd have to cadge them, or nick them.

I tossed a coin. Then I fetched Oddly's coat.

"Come on, Oddly," I said. "We're going to grovel to Keith."

Keith is not exactly my friend. In fact, he's not exactly a person. He is a walking advert. He has Adidas across his sweatshirt, Puma down his track bottoms, Reebok over his shoes, and Le Coq Sportif on his sports bag. His first word wasn't Mama or Dada, but Coca-Cola. His house is like a department store and his room is like Mission Control. It's a fair bet he'll have four HP11 batteries.

"Look who it isn't," he says, when he sees me. Then he realizes Oddly is with me. Suddenly he's my best mate. Keith has been bugging me to bring Oddly round, ever since I got him. Keith thought I was scared to bring him, in case he didn't want to go home again.

"Can I scrounge some batteries?" I ask.

"Sure," says Keith, but doesn't move. "Bring him in, then."

We go up to Keith's room. I pretend not to notice the new things that have sprouted since my last visit. Keith doesn't pay them any attention either. He only has eyes for Oddly.

"What can we make him do?" he asks.

"I don't *make* him do anything," I reply.

"What's the point of having a robot," asks Keith, "if you don't use him?"

"Don't talk about him as if he isn't here," I reply.

Oddly sits, sagging, like a sack of potatoes, just inside the door. We could probably talk about him till doomsday and he wouldn't react.

"Look at him," says Keith. "You haven't changed his clothes since you got him."

"He likes those clothes," I reply, although, to be honest, I've never asked him.

Keith fishes through a drawer and takes out a baseball shirt saying Dodgers. He pulls it over Oddly, then stands back to admire the result.

"There," he says. "Now he's
Somebody."

Oddly gazes blankly down at the
baseball shirt. He doesn't look like
Somebody. He doesn't look like
Anybody.

"Why don't you call him Clint?" says
Keith. "Or Zolph?"

"His name's Oddly."

"What a bore!"

"Can I have the batteries now?"

"In a second."

Keith sets off on a tour of the room, demonstrating all his latest toys. He puts a game on his computer and blasts a few Uglon Raiders. He runs his radio-controlled truck twice round the room. He switches on his keyboard and makes it sound like a piano, then a violin, then a fuzzy bee in a very distant bottle.

"You could have all these things," says Keith.

"Oh yeah?"

"Just put Oddly on show. Teach him a few tricks and charge five quid a time."

"I don't want to put him on show."

"All right. Take him down the car factory and see if they've got a job. That's where the other robots work."

Keith gets out his street hockey gear, and tells me why this or that is the smartest, hardest, wickedest, or dearest. But I'm not really listening. Over on the other side of the room, Oddly has come to life. He is leaning forward in his chair, mouth open, eyes glued to Keith's keyboard.

Keith yatters on. Oddly gets up and begins to creep very slowly forward.

"Can I see your bike?" I ask Keith suddenly.

"I'm showing you my skates," says Keith. He still hasn't noticed Oddly.

"I want to see your bike," I go.

Keith tuts. "Which one?" he says. "Mountain bike or BMX?"

"Both," I reply.

We go down to the garage. Oddly is left to his own devices, just as I wanted. A few minutes pass. Then a long single note blasts out of Keith's bedroom window.

"That's my keyboard!" cries Keith.

We hurry back upstairs. Oddly is marching round the room in frenzied circles, beating his arms up and down like a duck.

"Thanks," I say to Keith. "I don't think I need the batteries after all."

"It's that Dodgers shirt," says Keith. "I told you he wanted some new clothes."

Chapter Two

The moment we walk back into our flat,
Oddly wants to know when we're going
back to Keith's. I feel a twinge of
jealousy.

"You don't want to see Keith," I say.
"You want to see his keyboard!"

Oddly still hasn't learnt how to lie.
"That is quite correct," he replies.

"We'll go round when Keith's out," I
suggest.

Oddly considers this, then comes out
with his own suggestion, "Could *we*
have a keyboard?"

"Keyboards cost money," I reply.

"What is money?" asks Oddly.

"It's what you buy things with," I explain, then give some examples, which seem to confuse Oddly even more.

"Where is our money?" he asks.

"We haven't got any," I reply.

"Then we must ask for some," says Oddly.

I explain patiently that you can't just ask for money, unless you're the Queen. I explain that you have to work for it, unless you haven't got a job, like Mum and Dad. I explain that the more work you do, the more money you get, unless you're Keith's dad, who makes money by collecting rent, from people with no money like us.

"It makes sense really," I add, as Oddly starts to totter on his feet.

"There must be a lot of money in the world," muses Oddly, when he has recovered from his dizziness.

"Billions," I reply.

"Where do they keep it all?" asks Oddly.

"In banks, I suppose."

Oddly is very quiet after our conversation about money. I don't see him all afternoon, and I assume he's back in his airing cupboard. Mum comes back from the clinic, and I tell her all about the note that Oddly played on the keyboard. Mum tries to show an interest, but she can't see what will come of it. That is not surprising, because she can't see what will come of anything.

Just before tea-time, there is a phone call. It is the police station. They want to know if I have lost a robot butler called Oddly. I tell them it must be another robot butler called Oddly, not mine. Then I check the airing cupboard, to make sure. Oddly isn't there.

"I have lost him," I tell the policeman. "I just didn't know I had."

"I'm afraid I have some bad news for you," says the policeman.

"He hasn't been knocked down, has he?" I ask, panicking.

"He's been arrested," says the policeman.

"Arrested?" I gasp. "Why?"

"Attempted bank robbery," replies the policeman.

I put my hand over the phone.

"Attempted bank robbery?" I repeat, in a whisper.

"Well," says the policeman, "not exactly. He didn't have a gun, or anything like that. And he was quite polite. I believe his exact words were, 'I need some money. Please give it to me. I understand you have a lot of it.' Not surprisingly, the other customers panicked and threw themselves to the floor."

I hurry down to the station, expecting to find Oddly in tears. In fact, he looks quite pleased with himself, despite the fact he's in handcuffs.

"I'm on video," he tells me.

"Oh dear," I reply.

"And I've got a record," says Oddly.

"Yes," I reply.

"It's a police record," says Oddly proudly. "And the funny thing is, I don't even remember making it."

I try to explain Oddly's new interest in music to the police. They are even less interested than Mum. Luckily, though, they have decided not to press charges. They can't find a law which says a robot can't rob a bank. In fact, the sergeant is writing to the local MP, demanding a new law, in case Oddly tries it again. In the meantime, Oddly gets away with a good ticking-off.

"Have I done something wrong?" he asks.

"You could say that," replies the sergeant.

"Have I really done something wrong?" Oddly repeats, on the way home.

"Between you and me," I reply, "that's a matter of opinion."

After Oddly's adventure at the bank, it's clear I've got to do something. All right, we can't afford to buy a keyboard. But we could borrow one. We could borrow Keith's. Keith probably wouldn't even notice it was gone. What's that gap next to the stereo? he would think. Then he'd fill it with a new camera, or a drinks machine, or an electric guitar.

So I make another visit. I find Keith in his front garden, shooting gnomes with his laser gun.

"I knew you'd be back," he says, seeing me.

"Oh yeah?" I go, all innocent.

"I know what you've come for," says Keith.

Keith leads the way to his room, swaggering. He opens the door, walks straight past the keyboard, and picks up the Dodgers shirt.

"Cost us twenty," he says. "You can have it for ten."

Before I can think, I've taken the shirt, and I'm working out where I can get the tenner.

"Hang on," I go. "This isn't what I want."

"Don't be so selfish," says Keith. "Think of Oddly."

"It's not what he wants either!"

Keith snatches back the shirt. "What then?" he snaps.

"He wants your keyboard."

I didn't mean to blurt it out like that. I was going to do it in easy stages, e.g. "He wants your music book", "Oh, and he likes your keyboard case", "Yes, and, by the way, could you throw the keyboard in as well?" Still, I've said it now.

Keith smiles, a sneaky cat-and-mouse

smile. He runs his finger along the keyboard. "You are joking, I presume," he says.

"Go on, Keith. You hardly ever play it."

"How do you know?"

"You never talk about it."

"So?"

Keith is suddenly very interested in the keyboard. He switches it on and plays a few notes. "Tell you what," he says, "Oddly can come round here."

"Like hell!"

"Think I'm going to give it you, do you?"

"Not asking you to give it me. Just lend it."

Keith weighs me up. Something's ticking in his head. "How long for?" he asks.

"Ten weeks, say?"

Pause.

"All right then," says Keith.

"Ah, cheers, mate! We'll look after it, promise!"

"And after the ten weeks," adds Keith,

"I'll have Oddly."

My face falls. "No way," I reply.

Keith shrugs. "Hard old world," he says. "Don't get owt for nowt." He picks up a biro and chews it, like his old man with his pipe. "See you then," he adds, with a little wave.

I'm almost gone. But I can't bring myself to leave empty-handed. "You have Oddly for ten weeks?" I ask.

"A year," replies Keith.

"A *year*?"

"What have you got to lose? Oddly's as good as dead. He's dying of boredom, living with you."

"But you don't understand him. He's sensitive."

"Ahh!" says Keith, playing a make-believe violin.

"But he is! He can't control his emotions!"

"That's cos you've been too soft on him. I'll make a man out of him."

Keith begins to pack his keyboard. I don't try to stop him. He knows he's got the winning hand, and I know I've got to go through with this lousy deal.

Chapter Three

"Is it an ironing-board?" asks Oddly.

"No," I reply, "not an ironing-board."

"Is it a set of shelves?"

"No, not one of those."

"Is it . . . an unusually long cake?"

"Why don't you open it and find out?"

Oddly runs his hands along the case containing Keith's keyboard. Nervously, he unlocks the first catch, then the second. He lifts the lid. The next thing I know, he is clutching my ankles and frantically kissing my feet.

"Thank you, sir! Oh, thank you, thank you, thank you!"

With difficulty, I drag myself free. I tell

Oddly it was nothing, and what's more I'm Darren, not "sir". Oddly pulls himself together. He lifts out the keyboard and lays it gently on the living-room floor.

"This," he pronounces, "is even better than Keith's keyboard."

"Oh really?" I reply.

"Three times as good," says Oddly, "or possibly four."

"You reckon?"

"Oh yes," says Oddly, then adds, "I knew you had money really." He tries to give me a knowing wink, but Aunty Beth never programmed him for knowing winks. He strains and strains like he's got a fatal toilet problem.

"Shall we set it up?" I suggest.

We set it up: the stand, the keyboard, the mains lead and the holder for the music book. It ought to take two

minutes, but it takes twenty. Oddly is so
excited he screws everything I've
unscrewed, and unscrews everything
I've screwed. At last, however, we
switch the keyboard on, and all these
tiny coloured lights appear.

"It's like fairyland," says Oddly.
Aunty Beth took him to Tinkerbell's
Grotto once.

"Go on then," I say, prompting him
towards it.

Oddly lifts one finger. The finger moves slowly towards the keys, while the rest of Oddly backs away, as if he's expecting an explosion. Oddly gives the note a little tap. BARP, it says. Off goes Oddly, marching round the room, arms flapping, making smaller and smaller circles till he drops into a chair, exhausted.

"But how?" he asks, staring at his finger. "How does it do it?"

"Electronics," I reply expertly. "Like you."

"Can it make *your* finger make that sound?" asks Oddly.

I explain patiently that it was not Oddly's finger which made the sound, it was the keyboard. I prove this by playing the keyboard with my bum. Oddly is gobsmacked. He tries playing the keyboard with his nose, his elbow and

his foot. He still does his mad duck act,
but gradually it calms down, till only his
head goes round. Then he becomes more
like a dog, cocking his ear to listen to the
notes. He plays the very top note, and
shivers. He plays the very bottom note,

and laughs. He chooses other notes, like he's picking chockies from a box. Sometimes he hovers over one for ages, then chooses another at the last second. Sometimes he tries one, then puts it back. Certain notes become his favourites. He particularly likes the black notes, but too many make him feel sick.

Minutes pass, then hours, but Oddly doesn't lose interest. Outside, it starts to pitter with rain, then to patter, then to pour down. Oddly wouldn't have noticed if it was raining meteors. But I am starting to get itchy feet. I wander out along the corridor. Down at the lifts I meet Jackie.

You will remember Jackie. She was the one who re-programmed Oddly with feelings. Today, however, she is more interested in the waste chute. Instead of chucking a whole bag of rubbish down, she drops it piece by piece, so she can listen to it sliding thirteen floors to the basement. I get to see everything she's thrown away or eaten for the last fortnight. I'd prefer to live in ignorance.

"Oddly's playing music," I tell her.

"No he ain't," says Jackie.

"Yes he is!"

"Ain't."

"Is."

"Ain't."

"Is."

"Ain't."

"Is."

We always argue like this, and the loser is the one who drops from exhaustion. This time, however, Jackie decides to prove I'm right by seeing for herself. She makes her way into our flat, finds Oddly, and stands arms folded, looking critical.

"That ain't music," she says finally.

"It's robot music," I reply.

"It's got no tune," says Jackie.

"It's a robot tune," I explain.

Jackie points to Keith's music book.
"Play that," she says.

Oddly's finger freezes in mid-air. He
looks to me for help. "Ignore her," I tell

him. But Oddly likes to please Jackie,
because Jackie saved his life once by
giving him a cup of anti-freeze. So he
begins pressing his finger against the
book.

"You don't play the book, stupid!"
says Jackie.

Oddly's lip trembles. I tell him that

it's Jackie who's stupid, thinking he can read music when he can't even read books.

Jackie replies that it's easier to read music than read books. "All you need to know," she says, "is Eat Good Bread Dear Father."

Oddly's eyes begin to revolve.

"And FACE," adds Jackie.

Oddly begins to totter. Jackie huffs impatiently and stabs her finger at the book. "See these five lines?" she says. "E. G. B. D. F. See the spaces between the lines? F. A. C. E. See these tadpoles? If they sit on an A, you play A. If they sit on B, you play B. Easy."

I'm just about to say "Clear as mud" when Oddly says, "Thank you. Now I understand perfectly."

"Are you sure?" I ask.

"Quite sure," says Oddly. "So tell

me," he asks, looking at the keyboard, "which note is A?"

Jackie's face falls. "Hang on," she says, "I'll fetch me recorder."

We never asked for a recorder concert, but we get one just the same. Jackie plays the tune on page one, very slowly, with a few strange mouse squeaks thrown in. Then she sings it to Oddly:

> "Go and tell Aunt Nancy,
>   Go and tell Aunt Na-an-cy,
>   Go and tell Aunt Nancy,
>   The old grey goose is *dead*."

Jackie sings *"dead"* again, just to make sure we caught it, then smiles, showing her missing teeth.

"All we've got to do now," she says, "is find the notes on the keyboard."

Jackie starts searching for the notes. After a while, it is less like a search and more like a major expedition. I help out, except I'm even more tone-deaf than Jackie, and we squabble like chickens. Oddly leaves the room.

"See what you've done?" I go. "You've put him off!"

"He's got to learn properly," says Jackie.

"Why can't he learn his own way?" I ask.

"Just cos you can't do it," sneers Jackie.

I really hate Jackie sometimes. Especially when she's right. The fact is, I've always been able to teach Oddly everything, and I like the way he looks up to me. Oddly is the little robot brother I never had.

I decide to find him, and turn him against Jackie, and go back to how we were before. But he isn't in his airing cupboard. He isn't anywhere. Either he's robbing another bank, or he's run away to Scotland again.

"You've made him run away!" I yell at Jackie.

Jackie looks in all the places I've already looked, while I follow her around telling her I've already looked there. Outside it is raining so hard now that rivers are flowing across the car-park.

Toilet paper is streaming from the trees, and cans and bottles are being scattered to all corners.

"That's it," I say. "We've lost him for good this time!"

Hardly have these words escaped when the door to the flat crashes open. Oddly stands before us, drenched to the skin.

"I am sorry," he says, "but I am completely unable to find Aunt Nancy."

Chapter Four

When Mum and Dad get back, we have a good old row. Mum says we are cramped enough, without That Thing in the living-room. I ask what a living-room is for, if it's not for living. Dad decides it's a sitting-room. I reply that when Oddly was sitting, Mum told me to find him something to do. Yes, says Mum, but she didn't mean something that made a noise. I point out that everything makes a noise, even knitting. "Whose flat is this, anyway?" asks Dad. "The council's," I reply. By now I'm dangerously close to winning the argument, so Mum points out how young I am and how old they are, which means I shouldn't have answered back in the first place.

Oddly hates it when we argue. He winces as if we are hitting each other. By the end of the argument, he is standing there with both hands clamped round his ears. This gives me a good idea. I rummage around in the box under my bed and come out with a pair of headphones.

"There," I say. "Now he won't make a noise."

"He'll still be in the way," grunts Dad.

"We'll put him right in the corner," I suggest. "We won't even see him if we're watching telly."

Mum and Dad hum and ha. I plead and plead. Why can't they encourage Oddly for once, instead of putting a downer on everything?

"Anyway," I add, "it's only for ten weeks."

"Why is it?" asks Mum.

There is an awful silence. Oddly takes his hands from his ears.

"Cos . . . cos he'll be so good by then, he'll want to do something else."

Mum and Dad are beginning to waver. I squeeze my hands together in prayer. It always softens them up when I treat them like gods.

"Oh, go on then," says Mum.

"You're too soft on him," says Dad.

We park Oddly in the corner and arm him with the headphones. He seems happy enough, until he decides to talk to me, and yells so loud that everyone jumps six inches. I explain to him that we can't hear the music like he can. Oddly is amazed. He never realized what the headphones were for. He thought

they were to keep his ears warm.

As the evening wears on, Oddly begins to look frustrated. He turns the pages of the music book forward and back. He scratches his head. He sighs. I pull up a stool next to him and ask him how he's getting on. Oddly says that he's getting on well with the white notes, but badly with the black ones. The black ones don't seem to have names, like the white ones. Oddly is convinced they've been put there to confuse him.

"Will you help me?" he asks, full of trust and hope.

I study the keyboard. "Let's see," I mutter. I take up various expert positions, and put on various expert expressions. "Yes", I say, and "Mm" and "Aha". Finally I declare that the black notes are the ones you play at night. For the rest of the evening, Oddly doesn't touch a white note.

That night, I feel so guilty and ashamed, I can't sleep. I don't know if it is Nature that made me so useless, or Mum and Dad, or school, but I know there is only one person who can do anything about it. It's no good saying I'm a dunce at music and just forgetting about it. Music can't be that difficult. Keith can play it.

I get out of bed and creep into the living-room. I am scared. Not of ghosts, or diseases, or burglars, but of that little music book sitting on the keyboard. It's as if I can't even try to understand it. The moment I look at it, my brain turns into a blind lump of putty. But I *will* understand it, because I've got to.

I have an idea. I pretend it isn't a music book at all. I pretend it's instructions for building a model plane. I'm good at building models. So I start at page one and take it step by step. When I get stuck, I don't get angry with myself, I get angry with the cushion on the sofa. Three hours later, that cushion is in a bad way, but I have learnt where all the notes are, and the length of different notes, and what ♯ and ♭ mean. It was easy. I feel weird, different, and good. Also knackered.

Next day, Oddly is annoyed at me. He can't understand why I pretended I didn't know what the black notes were for.

"It was a mental block," I explain.

I remind Oddly about the mental block he had, that time he thought Aunty Beth's study was up the chimney. Oddly can't remember anything about it.

"That's because you've got a mental block about it," I explain.

Oddly is glued to the keyboard all day. He doesn't need a break, like us humans. I almost forget he's there. Then, half-way through *Brookside*, I hear a little sob. I turn to see Oddly, still in his headphones, shaking gently.

"Are you all right?" I ask him.

Oddly can't bring himself to speak. Instead, he points a shaky finger at the music book. It is open at "The Way We Were".

I hold one side of the headphones to my ear. Oddly begins to play. It is very slow one-finger stuff, but it is a tune. It is "The Way We Were". At least, it is the first half of "The Way We Were". At that point, there is a BLA-A-A-A-RT. Oddly's head has fallen sobbing on to the keyboard.

"It's . . . beautiful!" he wails.

"You reckon?" I ask, not being quite so moved myself.

"And I . . ." says Oddly, staring at his hands, ". . . I played it!"

"You did."

Oddly throws his arms around me. "Thank you," he cries. "Thank you for teaching me about the black notes."

"All right, all right," I say, not wanting Mum to be distracted from *Brookside*.

Come midnight, I creep out of bed again for my secret practice. I gently push open

51

the door to the living-room, and nearly jump right out of my jim-jams. Oddly is still at the keyboard. He looks like the Phantom Organist, just a black shadow, jerking with emotion. As I sneak closer, I see that the music book is still open at "The Way We Were", and tears are still rolling down his cheeks.

"What are you doing?" I whisper, tapping him on the shoulder.

Oddly recognizes me, dimly, like someone coming out of a coma. He looks around the room and seems surprised.

"Has everyone gone to bed?" he asks.

I point out the time.

"Oh," says Oddly, "I'd better stop soon."

I suggest that Oddly had better stop now.

"Just one more time then," says Oddly.

Oddly plays "The Way We Were" one more time, till that point half-way through when his head hits the keyboard. Then he wearily wipes his eyes, switches off, and comes to stand next to me at the window.

It is a clear night. From our flat you can see half the city, a thousand glow-worm lights, like a reflection of the stars.

We listen quietly for a while, to the
nightbirds calling, and the sirens wailing,
and some drunk yelling.

"I've got a plan," I say.

"What is this plan?" asks Oddly
eagerly.

"A concert," I tell him, "with everyone
we know in the audience. Aunty Beth,
Aunty Pat, Jackie and Aunty Linda,
and even some people who aren't
aunties!"

Oddly is knocked out at such a
thought. "And . . . and who will
perform at this concert?" he asks.

"You, you idiot!"

"Me? Oh . . . oh, I don't know."

"You can do it. You've only had that
thing two days and you can already play
a tune. By the time we have the concert,
you'll be a metro."

"A metro?"

54

"Or is it a maestro? One of those cars, anyway."

Oddly is lost, but gets the gist. He ponders a while. "And when will this concert be?" he asks.

"In about . . . ten weeks."

Something clicks in Oddly's memory. "Ten weeks," he repeats, as if it is a magic formula.

"Nine weeks five days, say."

Oddly looks at me curiously. There is a tiny doubt in his mind, like one of those tiny lights below us.

"You're not chicken, are you?" I ask.

"A chicken?" replies Oddly. "No, I'm not one of those."

"Will you do it?"

Oddly has another think.

"I will try," he says finally.

Chapter Five

For the next three weeks, Oddly practises solidly. True, he still only uses one finger. But that finger gets faster and faster, till it's keeping up with Mum's knitting, and Dad's nervous tapping on the arm of the sofa. Oddly plays "The Way We Were" twenty times a day, then thirty, then forty. A constant stream of tears rolls down his cheeks. One day he finally runs right out of tears, and steam comes out instead. We decide we'd better call for Aunty Beth.

You will remember Aunty Beth. She is Mum's sister, an inventor, in fact, the inventor of Oddly. At the moment, she is interested in solving traffic problems, and it is no surprise to see her arriving in her latest invention, the Gorilla Cab. The Gorilla Cab started off as a cable-car, like the ones they have in ski resorts. But it is no good having a cable-car without cables, so Aunty Beth invented a long pair of arms, so that the cab could swing from lamp-post to lamp-post. She is convinced this is the way to prevent traffic accidents, except those accidents people have by looking up at the cab.

The Gorilla Cab swings to a halt outside the flats, but it is not Aunty Beth who gets out. It is a butler, a butler like Oddly, except straighter, and neater, and not as confused-looking. You will remember that Aunty Beth gave us Oddly because she was inventing something better. Well, this is obviously the something. He doesn't walk round

the cab, he marches. He bows to Aunty
Beth, helps her out, and straightens her
hat. He opens the door to the flats and
waits for her to go in before him. Then
he opens a drawer in his stomach, takes
out a cake-tin, and follows.

"Isn't he smart!" says Mum, as Aunty
Beth introduces him to us.

"What's his name?" I ask.

"You and your names," says Aunty
Beth.

"He's got to have a name!" I protest.

"He's perfectly all right without one," says Aunty Beth.

"That's a good name!"

"What is?"

"Perfectly. Perfectly All Right."

Aunty Beth shakes her head sadly. "It was bad enough calling the last one 'Oddly'," she says.

I get a strange feeling that someone is behind me. It turns out to be Oddly. He's gone shy, but he's curious too.

"Speak of the devil," says Aunty Beth. She moves me aside and gives Oddly the once-over. "So he's still going," she says.

"Course," I reply.

"I thought he'd have gone west by now," says Aunty Beth.

"Oh no," I reply. "He did go North once," I add.

Aunty Beth peels back Oddly's hair and takes the cassette out of his head.

Oddly freezes in mid-movement. Aunty
Beth blows some dust from the cassette.

"Funny how these primitive things can
last," she says. "Just like that old Moggy
Minor I used to have."

Aunty Beth bangs the cassette back
into place. Oddly staggers around a
while, slightly dazed.

"So," says Aunty Beth, "he needs a
lachrymal refill."

"Do what?"

"He's run out of tears."

"Oh, yeah. I know his cassette goes in
his head, and his batteries go in his belly-
button, but I don't know how to fill him
up with tears."

Aunty Beth has a whisper to Mum.
Mum fetches a funnel and a length of
siphon tubing, and they take Oddly into
the bathroom.

"Can I watch?" I ask.

Mum blushes. "When you're older, perhaps," she says.

The bathroom door is closed and I hear the click of the lock. I'm left alone with Perfectly, thinking how stupid grown-ups are, and how boring Perfectly is. I wonder if I could secretly re-program him to answer back, or pick his nose.

By and by, Oddly is brought out of the bathroom. He looks rather ruffled, but Aunty Beth is satisfied he is back to normal. She and Mum start to chat, in the way grown-ups do, as if they've somehow forgotten you're there. Mum wants to know all the gossip, and how this person or that person's getting on. Aunty Beth hasn't got much time for this person or that person. She's more interested in why the toilet isn't flushing right, and whether it would be possible to invent a little robo-bug to clean the outside of windows. Meanwhile, Oddly sidles up to Perfectly, like a toddler who's made a new friend.

"Show him the flat, Oddly," I suggest.

Oddly takes up my suggestion. He is very eager to please Perfectly. He takes him to the bathroom, the kitchen and the bedrooms. He tells the story of his walk along the window-ledge, and laughs and laughs, and holds his sides. Perfectly stares blankly back. Oddly opens the airing cupboard door and proudly shows Perfectly his bed. Perfectly straightens the pillow and closes the door again.

Oddly has saved his best trick till last. He leads Perfectly into the living-room, busily removes the lid of his keyboard, and switches on the little coloured lights. Perfectly stays dead pan. Oddly points out the little coloured lights. Perfectly is still not impressed. Oddly gives a little cough, a musician's cough, and brushes back his tails, ready to sit on the stool. Perfectly moves him to one side, sits on the stool, takes one look at the music, then plays the whole lot, perfectly.

Oddly is devastated.

"Go on, Oddly," I say. "Show him what *you* can do."

Oddly backs away. There is nothing

I can do to make him touch that keyboard. He won't even admit he can play.

"He's very good, isn't he?" says Mum, of Perfectly.

"He's programmed to play music," replies Aunty Beth, matter-of-factly. "That's one of the improvements I made after the first model," she adds, looking to Oddly.

"Oh, but Oddly's been playing," says Mum. "Haven't you, Oddly?"

Oddly flushes bright green and shakes his head furiously.

"He can try, I suppose," says Aunty Beth. "But if you're not programmed, you're not programmed, and that's that."

"Would you like a scone?" asks Mum, noticing that the mood has become tense. "I made them myself."

Mum begins to prise the lid off her Tupperware box.

"What a coincidence," says Aunty Beth. "I brought some scones myself."

Aunty Beth opens the silver cake-tin Perfectly brought in. Inside are a dozen plump golden scones, with shiny tops and knobbly raisins bulging out of the sides.

"Great minds think alike," says Aunty Beth.

Mum quietly closes the lid of her own box. We eat Aunty Beth's perfect scones, while she has a quick look through the flat to see what needs fixing. Then she and Perfectly swing away in their Gorilla Cab, leaving all the household objects in perfect working order, and all the household people in ruins.

Chapter Six

I'm woken next day by the clink of dishes. Oddly is doing the washing-up. I think nothing of it at first. Then he starts on the hoovering. I begin to worry. Oddly hasn't been this interested in housework for a long time.

"Aren't you going to practise?" I ask him.

Oddly says he can't hear me over the hoover.

"Aren't you going to practise?" I ask again, when he's finished.

Oddly says he'll think about practice after he's done the dusting.

Evening arrives. Oddly has done the

dusting. He has also fed the plants, bleached the sink, done a red wash, a blue wash, and a bits-and-pieces greeny-orangey wash.

"*Now* are you going to practise?" I ask him.

Oddly sighs wearily. He says there are plenty of other things to do besides music, and just as important. He asks if it is fair to expect Mum to do all the housework. Then he collects three black bags of washing, and takes them down the launderette to use the driers. By the time he gets back it is past bedtime, and he says his batteries are too low for any more activity.

The pattern is repeated the next day, and the next, and the day after that. No matter how much work Oddly does, he can always find more. The dust on top of the curtain-rail, for instance. The little gap beside the wardrobe where the woodlice hang out. Not to mention the shopping, the cooking, and that little sticky ring under the bottle of cooking-oil.

Then Mum pounces. "Do you think we could have that thing out of the way," she says, "now that Oddly's lost interest?"

"I didn't think it would last," adds Dad.

I fly into a temper. I yell that Oddly hasn't lost interest, and they don't know anything about it, and they never wanted Oddly to play in the first place. Dad says "that's enough of that" and Mum says I don't understand the pressures they're under. So I say they don't understand the pressures I'm under, and Dad says what do I know about pressure, I've never paid a bill in

my life. Someone in 13–23 starts banging
on the wall, so Mum bangs back, while
Dad frog-marches me to the bedroom. I
go right under my duvet, and sulk, and
make the usual plans for leaving home,
etc.

As sulks go, it is not one of the best. I
try to hate myself and everyone else, but
half-way through I get a good idea which
may solve all my problems. I creep out of

bed and check that everyone else is asleep, because by now it's after midnight. Then, very quietly, I set about any little job Oddly has left undone. By the time I have finished, there is not one object out of place, one crumb on the kitchen floor, or one lurking germ down the lav. The flat is more perfect than Perfectly.

Next morning, Oddly is walking up and down the hall, scratching his head.

"Looking for something to do?" I ask.

"Ah," he says, having a thought. "The window-boxes."

"Already watered," I tell him.

"And weeded?"

"And weeded."

Oddly thinks again. "What about the bathroom taps?" he asks.

"Cleaned," I reply.

"And polished?"

"And polished."

Oddly is worried, but not quite beaten. "Of course," he says. "The rubbish."

I strut into the kitchen, where the empty bin is waiting, complete with fresh bin-liner. "This rubbish, you mean?" I ask cockily.

No reply. Oddly isn't there. In fact, he isn't anywhere. Blow me if he hasn't vanished again. I search the corridor, the lifts, even Jackie's flat. Then I catch sight of him down in the car-park. He is dragging one of the giant wheelie-bins from the basement, with the whole of Meadow Court's rubbish inside.

I take up the chase. I catch him half-way across the rec. "You're being stupid!" I cry.

Oddly stops. "Yes," he says. "Stupid. That's me."

"I know what you're doing," I tell him. "I know you're avoiding it."

"Avoiding what?" asks Oddly.

"You know what. The keyboard."

"I dusted it only yesterday," says Oddly.

"Stop acting thick!" I cry.

"Acting?" replies Oddly. "Who says

I'm acting? I can't act. I can't do
anything, except what I'm programmed
to do.''

I bang my head on the bin in
frustration. "I *knew* you were thinking
that," I go.

Oddly slumps to the ground and
squats there like a frog. His eyes begin to
brim. "Why did you show me that
keyboard?" he blubs. "I was all right
before that.''

"You were not," I reply.

"At least I didn't *want* anything," says Oddly.

"Yes," I reply. "You were like . . . a robot!"

"I'm still a robot," says Oddly. "An inferior robot."

"You're not inferior! You were doing brilliant till . . . you know."

Oddly hangs his head. "I'll never be as good as Perfectly," he says.

"Perfectly's rubbish," I reply. "He should be in this bin. When he plays music, it's just notes. When you play, you put over your feelings."

"If I put over my feelings," says Oddly, "you would know what I feel. And you don't. You never will. Everything you want to do, you just do, because you know everything."

I realize that the time has come, the time I have put off for so long. The time to tell Oddly that I am not quite as great as he thinks I am. So I sit down next to him, and let the truth come out, as easy as turning on a tap. I tell him about the time I got my width badge for swimming, by keeping one foot on the bottom. I tell him about the time everybody laughed at me because I thought the Alps were a pop group. I describe how I crept out of bed that night, and studied the music book, and learnt what the black notes were for.

Oddly refuses to believe a word of it.

I carry on, telling him the most embarrassing mistakes I've made, things I've never told anyone. I tell him about the time I let in nine goals for the Ruby Street Junior School second eleven. I tell him how I never sung a note in assembly, and all the excuses I made to the teachers, just like the excuses Oddly was making.

Gradually Oddly realizes I am telling the truth. A terrible look comes over him, anxious and careworn. His whole body seems to sink, as if a heavy weight has been loaded on to his shoulders.

"But . . ." he stammers, ". . . if you don't know everything, how can you tell me what to do?"

"I can't," I reply. "Not always."

"Then . . . I shall have to think for myself," says Oddly, looking more desperate by the second.

"I suppose so," I reply.

Oddly shakes his head. "I'm not sure I'm programmed to do that," he says.

For a long, long while, Oddly sits very still, just staring, trying to come to terms with the new situation. Then, wearily, he struggles to his feet, and begins to push the giant metal bin back towards the flats. That night, he is back at his keyboard, and practising harder than ever.

Chapter Seven

Oddly doesn't improve in a straight line.
He improves in bumps and jerks, one
step backwards, three steps forward.
Sometimes he goes a week without
making progress. Then, suddenly, he
makes a breakthrough. One day, for
instance, I find him studying a spider.

He watches it moving, then tries to copy it with his own hand. Later in the day, he is spider-walking his hand along the keyboard.

"Do you know what a chord is?" he asks me.

"I did," I reply, "but I've forgotten."

"It's one of these," says Oddly, and plays three notes together.

"Oh, *that* kind of chord," I reply.

Another time, Oddly and I are out for a stroll, when Oddly tells me something that's been bothering him.

"I don't think I'll ever play with two hands," he says.

"Why not?" I ask.

"Because," says Oddly, "when I'm thinking what the right hand should do, the left hand stops. Then I start thinking what the left hand should do, and the right hand stops."

"That is a problem," I admit.

"I can't see how you can do two different things at the same time," says Oddly.

I ponder on this.

"You're doing two things now," I tell him.

"Am I?" says Oddly, much surprised.

"You're walking down the road," I go, "and you're talking."

"So I am," says Oddly. He stops. "Now you've pointed it out," he says, "I'm not sure I can do it."

I tell Oddly about the time I tried to think about breathing, and discovered I couldn't, and spent the whole morning in the medical room. Oddly thinks this is hilarious. He decides he can walk and talk after all. We try adding other things, like wiggling our hips, and shaking our heads, and running a stick along the railings. Then we hurry back to Meadow Court before the men in white coats can take us away. Oddly is soon playing with two hands.

The day of the concert draws closer. Oddly begins to show signs of nerves. He spends a lot of time on the toilet, which is particularly worrying, as Oddly doesn't go to the toilet at all normally. He begins to bite his nails, except his nails are twice as hard as his teeth, so his nails stay the same length and his teeth get shorter. He starts to imagine things going wrong, really stupid things, like a power cut. He worries that he will have one of those mental blocks and forget where the D note is, or the A note is, or the keyboard is.

Mum and Dad begin to pull behind him. They've watched him struggle so hard, he's won them over. They start to offer little words of encouragement, like "I almost recognize that tune" or "You're really not that bad for a robot, Oddly". It may not seem much from some parents, but from mine it is a miracle. It goes against their deepest belief, that Everything Is Doomed To Fail.

But something else besides nerves is bothering Oddly. As we reach the last two weeks before the concert, he starts snooping round the house, looking at the telephone pad, and the bits of paper in the waste-bin. He wants to know who I've visited. He asks how many chairs we'll need, and how many vol-au-vents we'll be making. In fact, he really irritates me. Several times I come close to losing my temper with him.

It is not till the very eve of the concert that I discover what the problem is. It's well after midnight, and I'm sound asleep, when I'm suddenly woken by the bedside light shining into my face. Oddly is looming up behind it.

"Excuse me," he says.

"Why aren't you in bed?" I snap. "It's the big day tomorrow!"

"I wondered if I might see the invitation list," says Oddly.

"Is that what you've woken me up for?" I fume.

"It is," replies Oddly.

I sit up. I list every single person who has been invited, from Aunty Pat to the lad who lent me his Yo-Yo last Christmas. Oddly listens carefully. Then he asks again if he can see the list.

"I've just told you!" I hiss.

"But you might have forgotten somebody," says Oddly.

Oddly's been like this ever since he realized he had to think for himself. He's gone from trusting my every word to questioning every tiny thing I say. If I tell him it's half past ten, he wants to see my watch. If I mention in passing that it looks like rain, he goes to the window and studies the clouds. I'm surprised he hasn't asked for my birth certificate, to check my name really is Darren.

"Is there anyone in particular," I ask, "you think I might have forgotten?"

Oddly comes over all awkward. I try to remember if there's any girl he's funny about. Then, suddenly, I catch on.

"You wouldn't be thinking of Aunty Beth," I ask, "or her new butler?"

Oddly's head vanishes under the duvet.

"Relax," I tell him. "They're not coming."

One eye reappears. "Are you sure?" asks Oddly.

"I somehow managed to miss them off the list," I reply.

The rest of Oddly's head emerges. He seems much more relaxed now. "Could I . . . just check the list?" he asks.

"For God's sake!" I cry. "Just go to bed!"

Oddly makes a quick exit, closely followed by my pillow.

When I've calmed down, I feel sorry that I've lost my temper with Oddly. Like I said, he's been annoying me for a while. But it wasn't really the strange behaviour that bothered me. Or the constant questions. It was the fact that he is my best friend, and very soon, he will not be there.

Chapter Eight

I make up to Oddly in the morning. I get
him breakfast-in-airing-cupboard (a spot
of axle-grease and a small cupful of anti-
static fluid). We talk.

"Have you got butterflies?" I ask.

"No," says Oddly. "Do I need them?"

I try again.

"Are you nervous?" I ask.

"Oh yes," says Oddly. "I think I need
the toilet."

"Course you don't," I tell him firmly.
"Listen, all you've got to do tonight is
what you do every day."

"That's true," says Oddly happily.
Then his smile fades and he scratches his

head. "What do I do every day?" he
asks.

"Relax!" I go. "It'll just come, you'll
see!"

"Let's hope so," says Oddly. He
chuckles weakly. "I expect we'll be
laughing about it tomorrow, when things
are back to normal."

"Hang on," I go. "I think I need the
toilet."

Luckily, there is plenty to do, which
takes Oddly's mind off the concert, and
my mind off what will happen after.
Mum and I slice up the malt loaf and
measure out the orange squash. Dad
collects all the chairs in the flat (five),
then all the chairs in Jackie's flat as well.
Jackie decides to bring round their
standard lamp for a spotlight. Oddly
practises bowing in front of the mirror.
Everyone is alive and chatty, and our

boring old flat is full of the magic of
Something Happening.

Just before tea-time, there is a loud
BEEP from the car-park below. Jackie
runs to the window and does a little
dance. Aunty Pat has arrived. You will
remember Aunty Pat, who took us to
Scotland in Snowdrop, her warehouse-
sized lorry. Since then, Aunty Pat has
gone Green, because she is worried
about pollution. She has converted her

lorry to run on chicken-dung, and now calls it Snowdroppings. It works just as well, but now she has to keep a chicken-house, even bigger than the lorry.

"How's things?" she asks us. Jackie and I answer that things are fine, but Oddly isn't sure which things we're talking about, so he simply hugs Aunty Pat, and comes away covered in oil. Luckily he is wearing his Dodgers shirt while his best one is being ironed.

Aunty Pat is just the person we need to see. When she realizes how nervous Oddly is, she offers to drive us out to Ockiefield Lakes, so he can get away from the pressure. We climb up into the cab and count her new window-stickers, such as BULGARIA, MEXICO CITY, KUALA LUMPUR and WHITLEY BAY. We play the number-plate game, and a new game called Pub Leg Spotting, which involves spotting pubs and counting the number of legs in their name. For instance, the Green Man is two, and the Red Lion is four. It is neck and neck all the way to Ockiefield Lakes, till Oddly spots The Charge of the Light Brigade.

We find a nice patch of grass at the lakes, under the trees, by the barbecue area. Jackie feeds the ducks, I feed the swans, and Oddly feeds the radio-controlled boats. Jackie decides that Oddly needs to run off his nerves so she takes him on a jog round the biggest lake. Oddly comes back just as nervous as before, only exhausted as well. Jackie says that she is Supergirl, and Aunty Pat is Supertrucker, and Oddly is Supernose, and I am Super-can't-think-of-anything.

We remember all about our adventure in Scotland. For everything I say, Jackie says "Oh yeah! I remember *that*!" Even when I make things up, Jackie remembers them, and sometimes adds a few details of her own. Oddly is gobsmacked by it all, because he only has a 4K memory and there is a big gap in it, starting at Gretna Green and ending at the M6 junction on the way home.

After a while, things go quiet. Oddly's eyes begin to wander, like a dog hearing something far away.

"I have a strange feeling," he says.

"What kind of feeling, Oddly?" asks Aunty Pat.

"I don't know," says Oddly.

"It's the concert, I expect," says Aunty Pat.

"No," says Oddly. "It's something else. I've been feeling it for a while now."

"Maybe it's a change in the weather," says Aunty Pat.

"It is some kind of change," says
Oddly. "And I think Darren knows
something about it."

I freeze. Oddly waits.

"Don't be so silly!" says Jackie. "Come
on, everybody, we've got to move!"

Jackie and Aunty Pat are great with
Oddly on the way back to the flat. They
make loads of jokes, stupid jokes mainly,
the kind you'd normally sneer at. Jackie
tells him about the time she was Third
Shepherd in the school nativity play, and
how nervous she was, and how she
thought she'd never remember her line.
"What was your line?" asks Aunty Pat.
"Don't know, I've forgotten," says
Jackie.

We arrive. We can see people up at the
window, more people than there have
ever been in our flat. As we step out of

the lift, we can already hear the chatter and laughter. We walk either side of Oddly, like he's a champion boxer, or someone on the way to the gallows.

"You're going to blow them away, Oddly," says Jackie.

"That would be one way out of it, I suppose," replies Oddly.

The party is already well under way. Mum is dodging about, taking orders for squash and malt loaf. Aunty Linda's new baby has just been sick. Dad is lolloping about, doing his elephant impression. There is hardly room to swing a gerbil, let alone a cat.

"And here he is!" says Dad.

All eyes turn.

"The Organist Entertains!" says Dad, swooping towards us.

Oddly backs towards the door, but Dad is upon him. He puts an arm round

Oddly's shoulders. "This fellow," he says, "has been like a son to me. I won't say we haven't had our differences, but what counts is what you feel in here."

Dad bangs his chest. Oddly looks down at his own chest, rather confused, because that's where his spare shoes are kept.

"I'll be honest with you all," says Dad. "I didn't think he could do it. That old heap of spare parts play music? Never!"

I pray for Dad to shut up. Oddly's confidence is shrinking by the second.

"But I'll tell you what, ladies and gentlemen," says Dad. "He's proved me wrong. This fellow here is a Mozart. I promise you, you won't see a better concert tonight if you go to the Royal Concert Hall."

I make a mental note to hide the ginger wine, next time we have a gathering.

"Ladies and gentlemen," says Dad, "I give you . . . Oddly!"

There is a round of applause. Oddly steels himself, and with as much dignity as possible, picks his way through the bodies. Dad nudges me.

"Should've charged them on the door," he whispers.

"*I* wanted to introduce him," I mumble.

Oddly sits at his keyboard. He goes through the same routine as he goes through every day. He puts his music book on the stand. He switches on. He pulls back his cuffs. So far, so good. But there is a lot of noise outside, and Dad has left the window open. I thread my way across the room to close it. To my horror, I catch sight of the Gorilla Cab, swinging slowly but steadily towards the flats.

"It's Aunty Beth!" I whisper to Mum.

"So it is," says Mum.

"What's she doing here?" I ask.

"You left her off the invitation list," says Mum. "But luckily I spotted it."

Oddly finds his page in the music book. The crowd settles, till everything is silent. Oddly lifts his hands. The doorbell goes. Everybody laughs, because of the tension, I suppose. Dad makes a joke I don't understand, about "the bailiff". He opens the door. Aunty Beth walks in, closely followed by Perfectly. There are oohs and aahs. "Here's another one, look!" says Aunty Linda. "What can this one do?" asks someone else.

I glance nervously at Oddly. He is staring directly at me, with a look of hurt and disbelief. I shake my head frantically, as if to tell him it isn't my fault. Meanwhile, Perfectly takes his place in the front row, barely inches from Oddly's stool. "He likes him, look," someone says. "Maybe they'll do a duet," says someone else.

Gradually all becomes quiet again. But Oddly's hands have come away from the keyboard. He sits there limply, looking at the wall. "Come on, Oddly!" I whisper, between my teeth. But his face is vacant and stupid. The awful seconds turn into minutes, and there are coughs of embarrassment. "I think he's building up to it," someone says, and a few people laugh, but they know it isn't true.

At last, something happens. Oddly straightens, closes the music book, and switches off the keyboard. Then he stands. He begins to walk stiffly through the crowd, collecting coats and hats. At the hallway door, he stops and briefly bows.

"The refreshments will be ready shortly," he says. "I apologize for the delay."

Oddly leaves the room. Dad quickly leaps to his feet and offers a repeat of his elephant impression. I follow Oddly and find him in the kitchen. He is trying to act cool, except two glasses are already smashed, and the orange squash is everywhere.

"What are you doing?" I ask him.

"My job," says Oddly.

"No, Oddly!" I plead, snatching the squash bottle. "You've got to go back and play!"

"I can't," says Oddly bitterly.

"Just ignore him!" I plead, avoiding the word Perfectly.

"If you want me to ignore him," says Oddly, "why did you invite him?"

Desperately I explain what has happened, and how it isn't my fault. I remind Oddly of what I told him before, that his music is brilliant, because it expresses his feelings.

Oddly listens with a frosty face. "But I haven't got any feelings," he replies.

"Of course you have."

"No," says Oddly. "They've gone."

We stand there like strangers. Suddenly there seems no point in anything any more. Then the kitchen door opens, both of us turn, and there stands Keith.

"All packed?" he says.

This is the moment I've been trying not to think about.

"Packed?" asks Oddly.

"Mind you," says Keith, "I don't suppose you've got much to pack really, have you? Oh, and you might as well know, you're Zolph from now on."

"Zolph?" asks Oddly.

"Sounds more robotic than 'Clint'," says Keith. "Talking of robotics, I've done this deal with this DJ. He's going to pay a tenner an hour for you to body-pop down the Astoria."

"Body-pop?" asks Oddly.

"It'll make a nice change for you," says Keith. "Especially after making my breakfast, pressing my clothes, tidying my bedroom, cooking tea, and clearing up after me in the bathroom."

Oddly looks at me, expecting an explanation.

"I know it seems a lot," adds Keith, "but it's only what me mum does."

Awkward silence.

"I've changed my mind," I go.

Keith shakes his head. "*Oh* no," he says. "You don't go back on a deal."

"Deal?" asks Oddly.

"Hasn't he told you?" asks Keith.

Oddly looks to me again.

"Oo, you naughty boy!" says Keith. "Didn't you tell him how you got the keyboard?"

Just ten weeks too late, I give Oddly the whole story. As I do so, I begin to get upset, because I really was trying to do the best thing, and if it wasn't for Money, none of this would have happened. Everything is so unfair, and it's not my fault, and now Oddly will probably never forgive me.

A little tear comes to my eye. I wipe it away furiously. Oddly has never seen me cry, and I never wanted him to. His mouth drops open, his lip starts to tremble, and he begins to whimper like a puppy. He turns one way, then the other, as if he doesn't know what to do with himself. Keith backs away, afraid. Suddenly Oddly crashes past both of us and out of the kitchen.

"What's he gonna do?" gasps Keith.

"I don't know!" I gasp back.

Our question is soon answered. The air is filled with music, intense music, full of pain and pleasure and Oddliness. We hurry through to the living-room, where the Phantom Organist plays wildly at his keys, and the paper tissues are already on their way round the audience. Oddly hardly plays a bum note, and when he does, no one notices. Oddly has made the keyboard speak. It is one of the greatest concerts of all time, and when it finally ends, the living-room looks like a battlefield. Bodies are strewn everywhere, moaning and groaning and blubbing and saying they haven't enjoyed themselves so much for years.

Aunty Pat and Jackie shake Oddly's hand, give him a hug, and tell him they knew he could do it. Oddly closes his

music book, turns off the keyboard, and briefly cools his nose in a glass of squash. He seems tired, but strangely calm. Mum and Dad come up and say that he's reminded them of their honeymoon.

"You know, I wouldn't mind having a little go," says Mum. For the first time, she and Dad try out a few notes themselves.

I wait until things have calmed down, then go to offer my own congratulations. No one else realizes, but it is also my farewell.

"I'll come and visit you," I say. "Every Sunday."

"No you won't," replies Oddly.

"Why do you say that?" I ask.

"Because I'm not going," replies Oddly.

Keith frowns. "We made a deal," he says.

"No we didn't," says Oddly.

"Me and Darren, I mean," says Keith.

"Exactly," says Oddly.

I can't believe it's Oddly speaking. He seems so confident.

"It's not up to Darren where I live," says Oddly. "It's up to me. Didn't that occur to you?"

Keith is lost for words. It didn't occur

to him for one second. Or me, but that's another matter.

"The thing is, Oddly," I say softly, "we did have the keyboard."

Oddly is unmoved. "Keith has lots of things," he says. "We haven't got anything."

"But I gave my word, Oddly. I can't go back on my word."

It's an impossible situation. Even if Oddly does stay, there's no way Keith will let us keep the keyboard. But what would a story be, without an Aunty to step in and solve all the problems?

"I think I may have the answer," says Aunty Beth.

We are all ears.

"I thought that Perfectly was Progress," says Aunty Beth. "But now I see I have gone backwards. After all, the purpose of a robot is to make life worth living. I shall have to go back to the drawing-board and try again."

"Are you saying I can have *him*?" asks Keith, meaning Perfectly.

"Why not?" says Aunty Beth.

"Ah, wicked!" cries Keith. He looks Perfectly up and down, eyes on stalks.

"So we keep the keyboard?" I ask Keith.

Keith is stumped. It's a real struggle for him. He's never given anything away in his life.

"What would I tell Mum?" he asks.

"Tell her you swapped it for Perfectly," I suggest.

"Yeah," says Keith, "I could tell her that, I suppose."

We wait.

"Go on then, you have it," gabbles Keith.

"Cheers, Keith," I go, shaking his hand. "You're a pal."

"Yeah," says Keith, looking quite pleased with himself. "Suppose I am, really."

"How about another tune?" suggests Aunty Beth.

"All right," says Oddly.

"Yeah," I go, "but not 'The Way We Were', eh?"

Oddly looks quite hurt.

"I didn't want to tell you," I say, "but you've really got to improve your taste, Oddly."

Oddly nods. "I'm glad you're being honest at last," he says. Then he switches on the keyboard, doesn't bother to open the music book, and plays robo-music till our feet are sore from dancing, our throats are sore from robo-singing, and our ears are humming and buzzing from the Melody of Oddly.